ALEXANDRA'S SCROLL

ALEXANDRA'S SCROLL

THE STORY OF THE FIRST HANUKKAH

BY MIRIAM CHAIKIN

Illustrated by **Stephen Fieser**

HENRY HOLT AND COMPANY

NEW YORK

Henry Holt and Company, LLC
Publishers since 1866
115 West 18th Street
New York, New York 10011
www.henryholt.com

Henry Holt is a registered trademark of Henry Holt and Company, LLC
Text copyright © 2002 by Miriam Chaikin
Illustrations copyright © 2002 by Stephen Fieser
All rights reserved.
Distributed in Canada by H. B. Fenn and Company Ltd.

Library of Congress Cataloging-in-Publication Data
Chaikin, Miriam.
Alexandra's scroll: the story of the first Hanukkah / by Miriam Chaikin;
illustrated by Stephen Fieser.
p.   cm.
Summary: Alexandra, a young Jewish girl from Jerusalem, describes her
life and the creation of Hanukkah, more than 2,000 years ago.
[1. Hanukkah—Fiction. 2. Jews—History—586 B.C.–70 A.D.—Fiction.]
I. Fieser, Stephen, ill. II. Title.
PZ7.C3487Al 2001 [Fic]—dc21   00-40984

ISBN 0-8050-6384-6
First Edition—2002
Book design by Trish P. Watts
Printed in Hong Kong
10 9 8 7 6 5 4 3 2 1

To Shosh and Nehemiah Shlam
with love,
from the mother of the couple
—M. C.

To Jaime, Jodi, Joshua, Jill,
Emma, Michelle and David
with love,
from their uncle
—S. F.

Contents

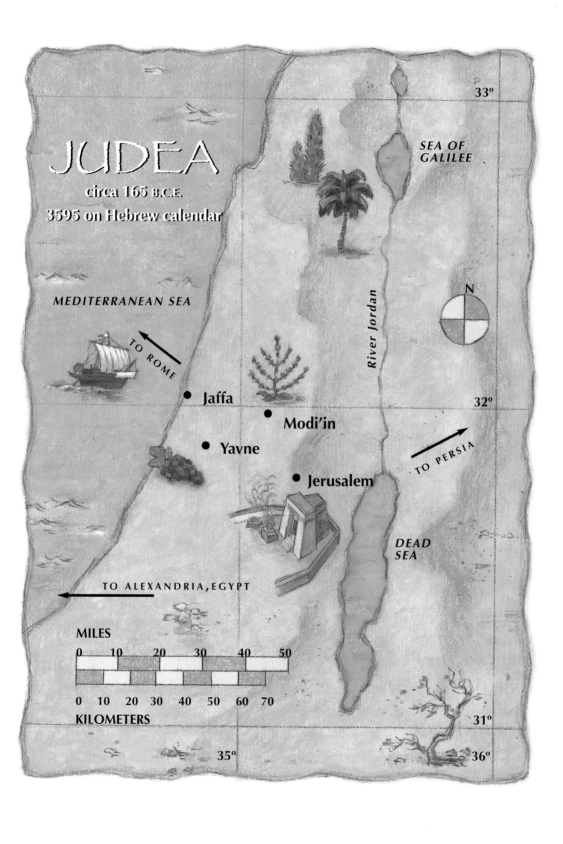

JUDEA

circa 165 B.C.E.

3595 on Hebrew calendar

MEDITERRANEAN SEA

SEA OF GALILEE

River Jordan

N

TO ROME

• Jaffa

• Modi'in

• Yavne

TO PERSIA

• Jerusalem

DEAD SEA

TO ALEXANDRIA, EGYPT

MILES

0   10   20   30   40   50

0   10   20   30   40   50   60   70

KILOMETERS

33°

32°

31°

35°

36°

Note from the Author

In this novel, Alexandra, a young girl living in Jerusalem some two thousand years ago, writes about her life. She, her family and her friends are inventions of the author. The historic elements in the story are the Greek-Syrian rulers of Judea, the laws against the Jews, the Maccabees and the rebellion they led for religious freedom. The historic story is told in full in Books One and Two of the Maccabees.

Alexandra's parents have taught her to write. She is upset and worried about the dangers in which the Jews of Judea find themselves. In an earlier time, Queen Esther wrote a letter to the Jews of the world telling them of the near-slaughter of the Jews of Persia. With her mother's coaxing, Alexandra is inspired by Queen Esther's letter to write about her own times.

The events Alexandra tells and writes about led to the creation of the Jewish holiday of Hanukkah, in 165 B.C.E.—3595 on the Hebrew calendar.

1

My Name Is Alexandra

My mother is the first one to say that nobody likes to live under a conqueror. Yet she named me Alexandra, after Alexander the Great. He was a Greek who conquered the whole world, as well as Judea, our land. My father wanted me to be called Ruth, after his mother, who lives in Egypt, but my mother won out. There is no surprise in that.

When I was small, my mother taught me to write letters on pieces of broken pottery. When I could write words, she and my father gave me a board coated with wax and a bone stylus to write with. It was a fine present. I loved pressing down with the stylus and seeing words appear in the wax, then lifting the wax, clearing it and starting afresh. I was soon writing full sentences.

My parents, and visitors to our house, often speak of Queen Esther. Storytellers in the market tell her story. She lived in Persia over a hundred years ago. She was a Jew married to the Persian king Ahasuerus. An evil man close to the king plotted to kill the Jews. He almost succeeded. But Esther managed to save her people. And when life was good again, she wrote a letter to Jews everywhere, relating the events of her time and warning Jews to be alert to danger.

We Jews of Judea are now in danger. The king has committed atrocious acts against us and our holy Temple. His soldiers fill our streets. His spies snoop in every courtyard. Thinking of Queen Esther and her letter, I began to wonder if anyone was writing our story.

I spoke of it to my mother, who was sewing at the open door, to use daylight.

"Queen Esther wrote about the troubles of the Jews of Persia," I said. "But what of us? Is there anyone writing about our times?"

"I don't know," she said. "But from the beginning of time our scribes have been recording our history. No doubt some scribe somewhere is writing about these times."

She bit the thread, separating it from the spool, and looked up. "Why don't you write it?" she said.

My mother delights in saying unusual things.

"I am not a queen," I said, annoyed.

She got up, taking her stool and sewing inside with her.

"You don't have to be a queen," she said. "You only have to know how to write and have something to say."

Something strange happened to me. It was as if a hand had come from outside, brushed away my annoyance and kindled a flame of excitement in my heart.

"There are no women scribes," I was surprised to hear myself say.

"Be the first," my mother said, putting away her sewing and bending to light the portable stove.

"I'm only a young girl," I said, joining her. She kneaded dough, pressed out flat cakes and handed them to me to slap down on top of the stove for baking.

"You know how to write," she repeated.

I felt strange to myself. I suddenly wanted to be the one to write the story of our times. Gladness filled me as I took the empty jug from the table and went down the stone steps at the side of the house to the courtyard, to fill it with water from the rain barrel. I glanced at my friend Rachel's door as I passed. Another time I would have gone in. Now, drawing water from the barrel, I was thinking of myself as a girl scribe.

When my father came home for the midday meal—he has a goldsmith's shop in the market—my mother told him about our conversation.

"Fine," he said as he ate. "I will bring a papyrus roll when I come home this evening."

Papyrus! My heart forgot to beat. Papyrus is paper made from a plant that grows in Egypt. It is for serious documents. You unroll it to write, then roll it up to put it away.

"And a reed pen and ink," my mother added.

"She can find a reed pen anywhere, and mix ashes, oil and gum to make her own ink," my father said.

"You can also buy it for her in the market," my mother said.

My father looked up.

I did not say anything. With my mother speaking for me, I did not have to.

"We have a scribe in the family," she said.

I could hardly wait for the day to pass. And when my father came home at nightfall and placed on the table a scroll, a reed pen and a cake of ink, I stared at the writing unit. It was beautiful.

"Well, Esther—" my mother said.

"My name is not Esther," I said, looking up sharply.

Our eyes met and we all laughed.

I did not want to wait. I wanted to begin writing now, so I would wake up in the morning as a scribe.

The door opened, and my friend Rachel came in.

"You are just in time to see a scribe at work," I said.

She looked mystified until I explained.

They all stood around watching as I took two oil lamps from their shelves and added them to the lamp on the table for more light. I opened the sheet of papyrus, put water into a small clay cup and set it beside the cake of ink. Then, seating myself on a stool, feeling important, I took up the pen and dipped it in the water.

"No," my mother said. "Add a little water to the ink cake, then pick up ink on the point of the reed."

I did that and held the pen in the air, not knowing where to begin.

"Well—?" my father asked.

"I don't know what to write," I said.

"You will think of something," my father said. "While you do, I will go down to speak to Simon Hasmon," he added, and left. The Hasmons were our neighbors downstairs, next door to Rachel.

"Tomorrow is the Festival of New Moon," Rachel said. "Start with that."

"It's customary to start with a little background information," my mother said.

I thought a moment and wrote:

Alexander was a good ruler, as my mother says. He did not try to stop us from being Jews. Although the whole world had taken up Greek ways and become Greek, he did not force us to become Greek. He let us keep our Sabbaths and festivals. Our holy place, the center of our lives, is the Temple of God, first built by King Solomon. When Alexander was in Jerusalem, he visited the Temple and sacrificed to God, to show respect for our ways. My mother says he was a man of learning and refinement.

My mother leaned over to read. Most of this scroll has been written with my mother in that position.

"Say a little more, to bring it up to our times," she said.

I wrote further:

My mother does not have a good opinion of the king who rules us now. He is a Syrian Greek, and the opposite of Alexander. He burned our holy books, killed our people and put up a Greek altar in one of the courts of our Temple. He wants us to stop sacrificing to our God and sacrifice to Greek gods.

His name is Antiochus. His officers and soldiers call him

Antiochus Epiphanes—Antiochus the Divine. We Jews change the sound a little and call him Antiochus Epimanes—Antiochus the Madman.

My mother read over what I had written.

"That's enough for a start," she said. "Tomorrow you can continue with New Moon, as Rachel suggests."

2

A Surprise at the Market

The scribe—that's me—awoke the next morning, happy as always to greet a festival day. I rolled up my sleeping mat, set it against the wall and threw open my shutters. I am the lucky one in our family. The one window in our house is in my room. The other room, my parents' room, is dark. Wicks burn in clay oil lamps there day and night.

I stood at the window breathing in the good Jerusalem air. Winter was on the way, and already her cold hand could be felt.

I love the sight from up here on the second story. I can see the flat roofs of Jerusalem, the top of the Temple of God to the left, and below, in the courtyard, my beloved jasmine tree. My mother says it is a bush, not a tree. I sniffed, as if I might inhale its sweet fragrance. But there would be no scent until the warm weather set in and yellow blossoms appeared.

Lifting my eyes from my tree, I looked at the stone wall that hides our courtyard from the street. I could not see the two doors on the courtyard floor, under my window. Rachel lives behind one. Behind the other lives Simon, the man my father went to see last night. I could also not see the rain barrel.

Remembering it was a festival day, I quickly washed at my basin, dressed, swept my room and went into my parents' room.

My mother is always up before me. She had already swept and set her bed mat, and my father's, against the wall. I was surprised to find her sitting at the open door, weaving on her hand loom, and to see bread on the table.

"Good morning," I said as I sat down to eat, dipping my bread in a bowl of goat's milk. "You are not supposed to work today. It's New Moon. Women do no work on this day."

"The shawl I will wear to the Temple had a frayed edge," my mother said. "If I don't seal it, it will fray further. As for the bread, I saved two pieces from last night."

I knew the bread was stale from the taste.

"One piece for you," she said. "The other for Father. When you take him his midday meal, stop at the baker's and buy bread."

She nodded at the table, for me to see the coins she had left. I waited for Rachel to call up to me from the courtyard. She was going to the market with me. We went everywhere together. Her voice soon came.

"Alexandra!" she called.

I finished eating, put on my cloak, took from my mother the cloth that held my father's meal—bread, cheese, olives and a fig cake—and put it in the goatskin pouch around my waist.

"Daughter!" my mother said as I went to the door.

I knew what she meant and reached up with my fingers to comb my hair. I like my hair free, loose, falling where it will.

"The wooden comb I gave you would tame that field of wheat on your head," she said.

"I like a field of wheat," I said, hoping she would not bring up the hand mirror that she had also given me, to monitor the field of wheat.

"When you come back, I'll braid your hair," she said.

I nodded, adding the coins to my pouch. That was our agreement. On Sabbaths and festivals, or when we had visitors, I let her imprison my hair in a braid.

"Alexandra!" Rachel called again.

"Just a moment," my mother said as I passed her. She pulled the collar of my cloak, to set it more evenly on my shoulders. I hurried down the stone steps to Rachel waiting in the courtyard.

She was my opposite. Her cloak hung neatly; her dark hair was always combed, with a part straight as an arrow.

"How do you always look so neat?" I said.

"I comb my hair," she said, taking my hand and pulling me through the courtyard gate.

The market is at the other end of our street, away from the Temple and down the hill. It is always crowded. On a festival

day the whole world is there, along with their relatives and animals. When we arrived at the entrance, we could not see a way in.

I put my arm through Rachel's. "Come," I said, plunging her into the crowd with me. We half walked and were half carried by the crowd, past noisy banging from the blacksmith's and coppersmith's shops and the cries of merchants, water sellers, strolling carpet vendors, beggars and braying donkeys.

"Aside! Aside!" a herdsman cried, driving his sheep and goats past us to an open space where animals and pigeons were sold for sacrifice at the Temple.

We pressed back against the stalls to let the animals pass and, when they were gone, continued on our way.

"Uh-oh," Rachel said, pinching me.

I love Rachel, but her pokes and pinches anger me. Every time she wants me to notice something, she pinches.

"Rachel!" I said, letting her know the pinch hurt.

She pointed with her chin, and I looked to see what had caught her attention. A soldier was buying a drink from the water seller. The sight of soldiers makes her nervous. She has reason. Whenever the king harms or persecutes Jews, Judah Hasmon and his band of fighters strike back. Her father is a member of Judah's band. It is a secret. No one knows.

"So what?" I said, making light of the matter, pulling her along.

She missed her father. And worried about him. But I knew how to distract her. We passed the potter and the broken pottery he always tossed into a pile outside his shop. I let go of her arm and began to search through the pile.

Rachel joined the search. She could read but did not write well. Since I became a scribe, she started to practice, scratching out messages to me and her mother. She handed me a couple of flat pieces to write on. I tucked them into my sash.

"For my practice," she said, slipping a sharp piece to write with into her pouch.

I put my arm through hers again and walked on with her.

"I love a festival day," she said. "The crowds, even the noise."

"My mother says a festival day used to be more joyous before Antiochus Epimanes became king."

Rachel removed her arm from mine and stared at me in horror. I had used our name for the king, calling him Antiochus Epimanes, Antiochus the Madman.

"You will get us killed," she said in a fierce whisper, glancing around the market. "His soldiers and spies are everywhere."

I put her arm back through mine and walked on with her.

"You're right," I said softly, pulling her along. "But he is"—I whispered the word—"mad. Not only for what he does to us. My mother says he gives cities to his lady friends as presents. And he jumps up on the stage and dances with actors."

Rachel stared straight ahead, as if I had not spoken.

I pulled her close, out of the way of a man pushing a wagon of cucumbers through the market. "Look," I whispered. "He wants Jews to stop being Jews and become Greek. How can we be Greek when we are Jews?"

"All right," she said, staring straight ahead. "But don't say it."

Different sets of stairs in the lower market lead to different parts of the upper market, where my father has his shop. He makes beautiful brooches, Jerusalem-of-gold pins and other gold adornments. The stairs closest to his shop were a short distance away. Instead of going there, I turned up the set of stairs we had come to and pulled Rachel after me.

"Why here?" she said. "The stairs near the tanner are closer to your father."

"They're closer, but the stench of dead animal skins can kill you first," I said.

The upper market is cleaner, prettier and quieter than the lower part. The air is sweet with the smell of spices coming from open sacks. We let go of each other and walked along, glancing about, taking in the beads, necklaces, ankle bracelets, fabrics.

"Alexandra!" Rachel said, pinching me.

I looked up. "I see him," I said, rubbing my arm.

We were both shocked. Standing in front of my father's shop was Judah Hasmon, the leader of our fighters, disguised as a camel driver. His robe was stained and dirty, and he was covered with dust. Although his head scarf hid most of his face, we would have known him anywhere. Before the king's men started looking for him, he often came to our courtyard to see his brother Simon, and my parents and Rachel's. He is the king's enemy. Why was he risking showing himself?

He saw us, put a finger to his lips and nodded to us to go in. Eyes forward, we hurried inside.

My father and a customer, a soldier, were bent over the scales, weighing a gold pin in one dish against carob seeds of equal weight in the other.

I removed the cloth from my pouch and placed it on the counter. "Your meal, Father," I said in an extra-loud voice, to hide my nervousness about who was outside.

My father looked up. "Ah, my daughter and her friend Rachel," he said, speaking Greek. Greek is his market language. At home we speak Aramaic.

The soldier glanced at us as my father wrapped the pin in a pretty cloth and handed it to him.

"I hope your wife likes her present," my father said.

"She will," the soldier said, heading out.

We three—my father, Rachel and I—watched, relieved to see the soldier walk on without noticing the camel driver. I turned to my father to speak of Judah, but he silenced me, took each of us by the shoulder and led us to the door.

"Do not look right or left," he said. "Go home and make yourselves pretty for New Moon."

We stepped outside, walking stiffly, without a glance at Judah. Rachel was silent. I knew that seeing Judah made her think of her father and miss him all the more. I felt sorry for her and took her hand.

"Your father is a hero, the same as Judah," I said. "They are fighting for our freedom, and to get Jerusalem back for us."

"The Hellenists don't think he's a hero," Rachel said.

The Greeks call themselves Hellenes. She was speaking of the Jews who had gone over to the king's side—who have stopped being Jews and taken on Greek ways.

"Who cares about them?" I said. As she was deep in thought, I led her down the steps that would take us past the dyer. The stench of smelly dyes would take her mind off her worries.

"Uh—what are we doing here?" she said at the bottom of the stairs, holding her nose.

"Walk fast," I said, holding my own nose.

We hurried out of the way and saw a crowd gathering around a storyteller. "Let's listen," I said.

"No, we still have to buy bread," she said. "Besides, I want to tell my mother—you know—"

I did know. She wanted to tell her mother and brother that she had seen the man with whom her father spent his days.

"And my mother is waiting for me with a comb," I said, to make her smile, hurrying on with her to the baker.

3

Preparing for New Moon

When Rachel and I entered the courtyard, the door of Rachel's house flew open, and Tamar, her mother, and Boaz, her little brother, were waiting with news. It was better than the news we had brought. Her eyes shining, Tamar told Rachel that Judah himself had been there and brought greetings from Micah, Rachel's father—who was well, missed his family and sent all his love.

I wondered at Judah's daring, coming to our courtyard. The king's men know his brother Simon lives there. They keep a close watch on the house. But I said nothing. I didn't want to spoil the family's gladness. Micah is in hiding in the hills, with Judah's men. He is a scribe. If anyone asks after him, Tamar has one answer: Micah is in Alexandria, copying holy books for the Jews there.

Boaz looked at his sister. "Guess who's here, who will come to the festival with us."

Rachel turned to her mother for an answer.

"Mattityahu," Tamar said, nodding toward Simon's door.

That excited me, too. Mattityahu is Judah's father—and Simon's. He is an honored priest from the town of Modi'in. We are proud to count him as a friend.

"Come, Rachel," Tamar said, moving inside. "Let us change for the festival."

She turned to me and said, "Bathsheba is waiting to braid your hair."

I heard Rachel laugh as I went up the stairs. I don't know why the subject of my hair is a cause for laughter. My mother does not find it amusing.

At the sound of my step my mother called from my room, "I have already eaten. Food is on the table."

Still thinking of Judah, I sat down to eat.

"I suppose you heard about the visitor," I called to my mother.

"I did," she answered.

"He is the king's enemy. Isn't he afraid of being caught?" I asked.

"The king's men don't know what he looks like, and he's always in disguise," my mother said. "Besides, he knew his father was here and wanted to see him."

Soon my mother came from my room, all dressed and holding a mirror and a kohl stick. I knew she had been sitting on the chest in my room, using the light from my window so she could see to darken the lids of her eyes. She was tall and slim. In her white wool robe, with an embroidered belt around her waist and a matching headband, she looked beautiful.

"How nice you look, Mother," I said.

"You will look nice, too—when I braid your hair," she said.

She followed me into my room. I took off my daily robe and washed.

My mother opened the lid of the storage chest and handed me my white wool festival robe. I slipped it over my head and watched it fall neatly to my ankles. As I looked down at myself, seeing the graceful folds of my robe, I felt the festival day had begun.

Comb in hand, my mother seated herself on the chest, pulled me over and began combing my hair. I stood with my back to her, facing the open window. I could smell roasting meat— animals being sacrificed on the holy altar.

"These knots are stronger than the walls around Jerusalem," my mother said, grunting with each pull of the comb.

"They are not knots," I said.

"What are they?"

"Shapes made by the wind," I said.

She gave my hair a tug and started on the braid. "I have some pretty yellow ribbon—"

"No decorations," I said, interrupting.

"Plain as an unadorned sack," she said, annoyed.

We heard the front door click open.

"Jacob?" my mother called.

My father looked in.

"I understand you had a visitor today?" my mother called after him.

"She knew even before I got home," I said. "He came to see Mattityahu in Simon's house."

"Some new trouble?" my mother asked, finishing my braid.

My father went into their room to wash and change. "There is a rumor that the king has been killed in Egypt," he called in answer. "But let us not be too quick to put ashes on our heads. It's only a rumor."

The thought upset me. Ashes! For the king! "Ashes are for mourning a loved one!" I said. "If it's true, I will put a laurel wreath on my head—and even comb my hair."

"What will it mean, Jacob, if it's true? If the king is dead?" my mother asked.

My father came in shining clean and fastening his cloak at the neck. "I'm sure it's not true," he said. "I met Joshua on the way. He knew nothing of it. He would have known—"

"Father! You exchanged words with Joshua?" I said.

"Joshua is high priest. I had to greet him," my father said.

My family calls him Joshua, but Joshua now calls himself by a Greek name, Jason. He isn't a real high priest. His brother was. Joshua pushed his brother out and bought the title from the king for a bag of gold.

"You are too polite, Father," I said.

"He is high priest," my mother said, bringing in my cloak and her own. "Sometimes circumstances oblige us to do things we'd rather not do."

"I thought you hated the sports stadium he built," I said. "Athletes running naked there and throwing the discus, bowing to honor the statue of the Greek god Hermes."

"Most of the athletes are Greek," my father said.

"Some are Jews," my mother said, handing me my cloak to put on. "But let not the naked athletes spoil our festival mood," she added.

"Alexandra!" Rachel's voice called from the courtyard.

I went to the window. They were all there, dressed for the festival and looking nice—Tamar, Rachel and Boaz. Simon Hasmon, holding the new baby, and his wife, Sarah. Mattityahu, looking handsome and dignified in his silk robe, with his white beard combed and spread out on his chest.

"We're coming," I called down.

4

A Dark Day

We left the courtyard in a good mood, joining the happy parade of people in the street heading for the Temple. We walked in twos on the narrow street, Rachel and I in front, Mattityahu and Simon last, and everyone else in between. Cries of "Happy New Moon!" and "A good month!" filled the air as people called to each other. Many recognized Mattityahu and bowed to him in greeting.

"I'm taller," Rachel said, snuggling up to me, putting her shoulder to mine.

She was, a little, but I lifted my shoulder higher and said, "You are not." We laughed and began to skip.

"Walk properly," my mother called. "Like well-bred Jerusalem maidens."

Rachel and I looked at each other and laughed. We walked on, waving to friends, wishing everyone a good New Moon.

Rachel pinched me. "Look who's there," she said.

Her pinches hurt, and I would have liked to stamp on her foot, but I was curious to see who she was talking about. I turned to see Eliahu leave his group of friends and come toward us.

"A good month!" he called over our heads, greeting our parents first. "And to you, my lord," he added, bowing to Mattityahu.

They wished him the same.

He fell in beside Rachel and me. "Are you ready to dance with the moon?" he asked.

"Ready?" I said. "I must. Doesn't our religion teach us to serve God in gladness on a festival day?"

"Gladness means singing, too," Rachel said.

"Eliahu," Boaz called, "is that your pigeon being sacrificed on the altar?"

Boaz sniffed the air at the aroma of meat roasting on the Temple altar.

Eliahu breathed in, testing the air. "No, it's my uncle's goat," he said, laughing, and headed back to rejoin his friends.

Rachel made a noise as we passed one of the statues of Greek gods that Antiochus had put up around the city. "My mother explodes when she sees these," she said. She glanced back at her mother and made a face. Her mother made a face back and smiled.

Behind us my father was telling Boaz about New Moon festival.

"The moon is a symbol of our nation," he said. "It may disappear for a while, but it always comes back again."

"How can our nation come back?" Boaz asked. "We never left."

His mother, walking with my mother, answered from behind. "We are here, but we are living under foreign kings," she said.

"One day we will live as a nation again. That is what will return—our freedom."

Rachel and I, hurrying ahead, reached the steps of the Temple court first and waited for the others to catch up.

Rachel pinched me to call my attention to the Jewish boys wearing broad-brimmed Hermes hats, like the Greek god. The three men behind them were an even worse sight. Each wore at the waist a gold buckle, a signal that he was "a friend of the king." Some Jews who wear them are spies for the king.

"Did you see them?" I asked my mother.

"I did," she said.

Mattityahu glared at the backs of the men. "How dare they come to the Temple!"

"Pay them no mind, Father," Simon said. "Let us enjoy New Moon."

Hundreds of people were gathered under the open sky in the Temple court. As my father and Simon went to look for a good place for us to stand together, we watched the parade of priests on the ramp that led to the altar, some going up carrying bowls of water, others going down carrying away pans full of ashes. Sacrifice priests were busy at the altar, offering animal parts up to God.

My father came and led us to where Simon was guarding our place. It was a good choice. We had a fine view of the steps from there. Around us people chatted. Some stopped to speak with our parents, some to greet Mattityahu. A Greek friend of my father's, a merchant from the market, waved as he went by. Many Greeks came to the Temple on a festival day to enjoy the celebration.

"Here come the torch priests," Boaz said.

I became excited, watching the priests go with lit torches along the walls, touching their flames to the unlit torches fixed to the walls, throwing light on the court.

"Let there be light," I said to Rachel.

Rachel jabbed me, nodding for me to listen to her mother's conversation behind us.

I took Boaz by the shoulders and dragged him around to stand between Rachel and me. Let him catch the next pinch. I listened to the conversation Rachel wanted me to hear.

"And your husband, is he still in Alexandria?" a woman asked.

"He is," Tamar answered. "Many Jews want holy books of their own. He has much work there."

Rachel leaned around Boaz and whispered in my ear, "I'm beginning to believe my father really is in Egypt."

As our parents chatted with friends behind us, we three stood looking about the Temple court.

"So many doors," Boaz said. "What are they?"

"Some are storage rooms," Rachel said. "For musicians' instruments, priests' robes, grain and barley for the poor, a charity room, with clothes and linens for orphan brides—"

"One is our treasury, a secret room where priests keep the gold and silver of people," I said. "But no one knows which one."

I care more about the sacred rooms of the Temple, the Holy Place, with a curtain for a door, and the Holy of Holies behind a second curtain. Before the Holy Place was our seven-branched gold Menorah, our greatest treasure. It is from the time of Moses and the Israelites. Seven flames burned in each of the cups.

"I know what else is in the Holy Place," Boaz said. He had just started school and was proud of his learning. We let him tell us.

"The other holy objects God told Moses to make for the first house of God," he said proudly.

"What are they?" Rachel asked.

"A gold show table with twelve loaves of bread, six in a row. And a gold incense altar," he said.

Rachel and I looked at each other. He was right. But we didn't want him getting too pleased with himself.

"Do you know who bakes the bread?" I asked.

"I didn't learn that yet," he said.

"The Garmu family," I said. "Only they know the secret recipe."

"The incense is a secret, too," Rachel said. "Only the Avtinas family knows what herbs to use."

Boaz was not ready to let his star fade. "I know what's behind the curtain, in the Holy of Holies," he said. "Nothing!"

He was right again. The Holy Place leads to a curtain that is the door of the Holy of Holies, our most sacred chamber. When I first learned it was empty, I could not see how a room with nothing in it could be holy. When I asked my mother about it, she said it wasn't empty. "What is in it cannot be seen," she said. "It is God's spirit."

A loud blast of the horn announced the start of festivities for New Moon. I was well out of Rachel's reach when she cried, "It's starting!"

The court filled with excitement as priests in white linen tunics and white turbans came marching out, followed by musicians and singers in their white robes.

At a signal from the choirmaster, the chorus sang, *"In the courts of the Lord's house, in the midst of thee, O Jerusalem, hallelujah."*

I glanced at my mother behind me. I was happy for her. She loved the singing.

A musician priest gave three blasts on the horn as a sliver of moon showed in the sky. As we looked up at the sky, priests chanted: *"Blessed is the Lord our God, king of the universe, who with a word created the heavens and ordered the moon to renew itself. Hallelujah, O ye servants of the Lord, praise the name of the Lord."*

"Servants of the Lord" meant us—except for the gold buckle wearers—and we sang together, *"Praise the Lord."*

Then, with musicians accompanying them on harps, flutes and cymbals, the choir sang, *"Praise him from the heavens. Praise him in the heights. Praise him all his angels, sun and moon, all you stars of light, for he commanded and they were created."*

I closed my eyes and listened to my mother's sweet voice singing along with them.

Then came our part, the part children love most. The priests chant, *"May the Holy One, blessed be he, grant his people in this new month a life of peace, of goodness, of blessing, of health, a life that holds the fear of heaven, that is free of shame or humiliation, a life of wealth, honor and a love of God's law."*

When they chant, *"As we dance toward thee, but cannot touch thee, so may no harm touch us,* "we children stretch out our arms, holding up our hands to heaven, and leap into the air, dancing with the moon.

"Look at Eliahu," Rachel said, leaping, nodding to where Eliahu's head bobbed up higher than the rest.

Our parents bounced lightly on their toes.

As suddenly as two fingers extinguish a flame, the dancing stopped and joy left our hearts.

We heard the sound of thunder that was not thunder: the sound of horses' hooves and chariot wheels striking the paving stones. The king was not dead. Only he had chariots. When the chariots halted outside the court, we heard shrieks and cries of slaughter as the king's men killed whatever men, women and children were unlucky enough to be on the street.

All was terror and darkness. I could not turn my head, but I felt my mother's hands on my shoulders, trembling, holding me fast.

Torches blazing, Antiochus and his men stormed up the Temple steps with shouts. Some of his men remained standing in the court, pointing spears at us, as the king and others went up to the Holy Place and came out carrying away our gold Menorah, the gold incense burner, and every gold and silver cup and bowl. As they left, they unhinged the Temple door and ripped from the door all its gold decoration.

While the chariot wheels rolled away, there were more cries of slaughter. The horror was not yet over. The soldiers on the court floor went into a room of the court, came out with heavy sacks and left laughing.

"They are carrying away the people's gold and silver," my

father murmured, his voice heavy with anger. "Some Hellenist has revealed the location of the secret room."

Our hearts frozen, we stood staring in silence at the wretched sight—our beautiful Temple shamed, standing naked, scarred and forlorn.

Mattityahu's voice shattered the silence.

"O, woe is me!" he cried. "Why was I born to witness the ruination of my people and our holy city!"

5

The King Passes New Laws

No one was surprised when the king's guards were found dead. We had expected Judah to take revenge on the king, and he had. We went out very little. When I did go out with my mother, the soldiers in Jerusalem looked at us with suspicion, even hatred.

On the twenty-fifth day of Kislev—who can forget the date?—disaster followed disaster.

My mother and I were at home, weaving by the last rays of the sun, when my father came home with news.

"The king's men are going around the public squares reading out a new set of laws passed by the king," he said, his face white with anger. "It is now illegal for us to be Jews."

My mother and I heard what he said but couldn't believe it.

"Decrees are posted about the city—in Greek and Aramaic," he went on. "I have copied the accursed words."

He took from his pouch a piece of pottery and read:

DECREED BY ANTIOCHUS, KING OF GREEK SYRIA AND JUDEA, IN
THE ONE HUNDRED FORTY-FIFTH YEAR OF THE GREEK KINGDOM,

JEWS MAY NOT—
SACRIFICE TO THEIR GOD,
OBSERVE THEIR SABBATHS AND FESTIVALS,
READ THEIR HOLY BOOKS,
CIRCUMCISE INFANT BOYS.

WHOEVER GOES AGAINST THE KING'S LAW SHALL DIE.

It was murder. He was murdering our religion. We live by the laws God gave Moses for us to obey. From today, if we kept God's law, we would be killed.

We sat in stunned silence when the door opened and Simon Hasmon came in with more news.

"They have put up a statue of Zeus on our holy altar and sacrificed a pig on it," Simon said.

Here was another death, another murder. We are allowed to sacrifice only certain animals to God. Pig is forbidden. The king knows that. Everyone in Jerusalem knows our ways. He had polluted our altar. It was no longer holy. We could no longer sacrifice to God. He had stolen our way of life.

Simon sat down. "We are leaving with my father for Modi'in," he said. "Antiochus does not bother with small towns. We will be able to live as Jews there and be safe."

"When do you go?" my mother asked.

"This very day," Simon said. "Many are leaving."

My mother turned to my father. "I think we should go, too," she said.

This day was full of shocks. My father and I stared at her.

Simon said, "My brothers' houses are full. But my father is alone. If you decide to come, he has room for you."

"We will not leave at once," my mother said. "We will wait and see how things go for spring, after the rains. Travel will be easier."

"Is Rachel's family leaving?" I asked Simon.

"They will stay," Simon said. "The authorities know Micah is a scribe, and they believe him to be in Alexandria. We need people to stay, as a base, to collect information, and other things."

No date had been set. But even in my mind, I could not bear the thought of leaving Jerusalem, or Rachel. I looked at my mother. "Why must we wait and see? Why can't we stay and collect information like Rachel's family?"

"We will do what must be done," my mother said.

I did not like the sound of it. "But Father must stay in Jerusalem for his business," I said.

They looked at me in silence.

I was not ready to give up. "If you both must leave, I can live downstairs with Rachel," I said.

"If we go, we go as a family," my mother said. I knew that tone of voice. It was like an iron gate swinging shut.

Simon rose, nodded and left.

My mother came over and kissed me on the head.

6

The Rains

It is already a different Jerusalem. Joy is gone from our hearts and our streets. The weather cries with us. Heavy rains fall almost daily. The few times that my mother and I go out, we walk in pools of water or slip around in the mud. Now and then the rain takes a rest and the sun comes out, but before it can do its work and dry the mud, there is another rainfall.

"Come," my mother said one day when the sun shone. "Antiochus has no power over plants and flowers. Let us go draw nourishment from God's handiwork."

We spent a pleasant hour in a nearby wood, enjoying what my mother calls God's handiwork—an almond tree in bloom, a lovely lavender bush and cyclamen growing out of tree trunks and rocks.

My father brings us whatever we need from the market. We need little. Each day we bake our bread. My mother mixes flour and water and kneads the dough. I make fire in the oven. When the kindling burns down, I make flat cakes of the dough and

place them on the hot stove to bake. Our storage jars are full of grain, beans, lentils, oil, honey and wine for the Sabbath. We cannot celebrate our festivals anymore. Our Temple is no longer ours. The Sabbath we have to celebrate secretly and quietly, for some soldier or spy might be lurking in the courtyard. My father brings goat's milk and cheese and whatever greens he finds for sale. He brings me papyrus and ink. And he brings us news of the outside world.

There are battles between our men and the king's. More statues of Greek gods have been put up in the streets of Jerusalem. Soldiers live in our Temple and cook and eat there. They and the king's spies look for Jews who might be breaking the king's laws.

My father has told us of a man walking alone, talking to himself. Soldiers fell upon him, demanding to know if he was praying to God. They were ready to kill him until they realized his mind was not in order. My father has also told us a story that is hard for my lips to utter and my hand to write. My mother has forced me to write it. She says if I am writing about these times, I must be faithful to history and recite each event. She says Queen Esther did not leave anything out of her report. This is the hideous event.

The king's soldiers learned of two women who had circumcised their infant boys in secret. The soldiers killed the infants, tied them around the mothers' necks and paraded them around the city as an example of what happens to Jews who disobey the king's laws. They then took the mothers and dead infants to a roof and threw them down into the street. It is a bad time for us, a very bad time.

Another day, I again went with my mother to draw nourishment from the wood. Red flowers on the pomegranate tree and the sight of white broom brought joy to our hearts.

My mother said little, but I knew as she moved about the house that she was thinking of leaving when the rains were finally over.

Rachel and I play dice games every day, either in her house or in mine. Sometimes my mother tells us stories about our prophets, sometimes her mother tells us stories about Moses and others in our history. Boaz, Rachel's little brother, sits and listens. The rains have begun to lessen and the sun to come out more often and stay longer. I had been dreading the conversation that would come. And one day it did, while we were eating our evening meal.

"I cannot live this way," my mother said. "I cannot open a sacred book for fear some soldier or spy will report us. I cannot light candles on the Sabbath."

"Yes, it is difficult," my father said. "I live under tension in the market as well. My Greek friends are fine. But the soldiers, and the Hellenists, are eager to make trouble for us."

"I am a stranger in my own city," my mother said.

For a moment no one spoke. Then my mother looked at my father.

"We will leave," she said. "Send word to Mattityahu that we will be coming."

I was turned to stone. My mother looked at me. "I know you don't want to leave Jerusalem," she said. "I don't either. But we will not be away forever."

"For how long?" I asked, at the point of tears.

"I don't know, but kings come and go—" she said.

"Like the moon," I said, crying.

I ran down the steps to Rachel's.

Boaz was sitting on the edge of his sleep mat, which was unrolled on the floor. I told Rachel through my tears about the decision that had been made. We both sat down on Boaz's mat and cried. Boaz cried with us.

"It will only be for a while," Tamar said, bringing three earthen plates, each with a poppy-seed cake, one for each of us.

"Don't let the crumbs fall, or demons will come to disturb Boaz's dreams in the night," she said.

I looked at her. "Do demons eat the crumbs?" I asked, setting the plate carefully under my chin.

"They cannot leave the dream. They see the crumbs and try to get out to eat them, but they are imprisoned in the dream," Tamar said. "It is their pushing and pulling and wild movements that disturb the dreamer."

"Mother!" Rachel said, eating her cake. "You're making it up. Father told us there were no demons. He's a scribe. He knows what the books say."

Tamar sat down with us. "Alexandra, these are troubled times," she said. "We do what we must. Besides, it will not be forever," she added, sounding like my mother.

Her words made me feel ashamed. Rachel was doing what must be done, living without her father so much of the time, missing him. And Micah, her father, was doing what must be done, fighting at Judah's side.

I finished my cake, handed Tamar the empty plate and rose from the mat. I looked at Rachel.

"I miss you already," I said. "How will I live without your pinches?"

"How will I live without your arm to pinch?" she responded, tears coming to her eyes.

My eyes were also full of tears as I said good night and went up the stone steps.

"Maybe," I thought, unrolling my mat on the floor, "I'll get up in the morning and find that this day never happened, that it was all a dream."

7

Spring

It had been no dream. The next morning my mother woke me with the words, "We will leave in two days. Father is making arrangements."

I sat up, blinking sleep from my eyes. My heart was heavy. With the Temple ruined, and priests and Temple musicians and officials gone from the city, Jerusalem was no longer the same. Even so, I did not want to leave. I had never been away except when we went to visit relatives. And I had never been parted from Rachel except for those times.

"What will happen to our house?" I asked, rolling up my mat.

"Father will remain here," my mother said.

"But you said if we go, we go as a family."

"It has all been worked out," my mother said as I washed and dressed. "It is better if he stays. The authorities know he has a business in the market. They know him. They don't know us. One or another of Judah's men may stay here, when there is need. If Father is also here, it will take suspicion away from the house."

My heart ached. Already I could see myself gone from Jerusalem. I opened my shutters and looked out. The sweet smell of jasmine filled the air. I breathed deeply and wanted to cry. Now that my tree was covered with yellow blossoms and sending out perfume, I would not be here to enjoy it.

Oh—I was an unhappy scribe.

I ate the morning meal without speaking to my mother, then swept and went down to Rachel. She was as sad as I was. We played dice games and agreed not to speak about my going.

No one asked him, but Boaz also said he would not speak of it.

All too soon it was the morning of our departure. As I opened my eyes and glanced about, I saw a half-empty house. Shelves were bare. Bundles stood ready on the floor.

"Father has hired a chariot with ears," my mother said. That is her name for a donkey.

She spoke of our plans as I ate my bread and goat's milk.

"We two will leave as soon as you're ready," she said.

"What of Father?" I asked.

"I told you, he must stay. He will come for a visit in a day or two."

I watched her tie another bundle.

"It looks as if we will be gone forever," I said.

"There is no forever," she said. "See to your garments and fold them neatly in your cloak."

I went to my room and removed from my shelf a wool robe, two of cotton, a head scarf, stockings and underclothes, and folded them into a cloak. I opened the lid of the chest and looked at my white wool robe for Sabbaths and festivals.

"Should I take my festival robe?" I asked.

"Leave it here," my mother said. "Father will bring what we need."

Another wave of unhappiness washed over me as I assembled the wooden comb I never used and the mirror I never looked into, and slipped them into my rolled-up mat, along with the board for playing dice and the dice themselves.

I wondered if I would find friends in Modi'in.

"Are there children in Modi'in?" I asked.

"Simon has only the baby, but his three brothers also live in the town and they have older children," my mother said.

A donkey brayed in the courtyard, and I went to look out the window.

"Your chariot is here," Rachel called up from the courtyard.

Tamar, her mother, was speaking with the donkey driver, who came to take our bundles down.

When the last bundle was down, my mother left the house without looking back. I stood at the door, unable to take my eyes, or my self, from my home.

"Alexandra!" she called.

Unwilling feet took me down.

My mother filled the donkey's side pouches with the honey pot, flour jar, food for the journey and waterskins. The driver stood ready with his "talking stick," the thin branch he used to tell the donkey when to move and when to stop. The donkey did not always listen.

Rachel and I cried and hugged until my mother lifted me onto the back of the donkey. She kissed Tamar, Rachel and Boaz, then nodded to the driver. He touched the "talking stick" to the donkey's back, and we all left the courtyard, I on the donkey's back, and my mother and the driver walking on either side of the animal.

I knew Rachel had followed us out into the street. I did not look back. I would not have seen her if I had turned. My eyes were too full of tears to see anything. I raised my hand in the air and waved my fingers in a backward good-bye.

8

Modi'in

We—my mother—decided I should leave in Jerusalem the scrolls I have written upon, rolled up and stored in the chest. She says Mattityahu is a priest and scribe and will have papyrus for me to write on, until my father brings fresh sheets and a cake of ink in a few days. I can find a reed to write with anywhere. They grow near water, any stream or pond.

The way to Modi'in was hard. My mother, who always would sing on a journey, sang not a note. Unhappiness silenced us both. The driver and donkey also seemed unhappy. Every now and then the donkey refused to move, even when the driver applied the "talking stick." The man was obliged to get behind the donkey and push. When still the donkey refused, my mother helped, pushing from behind while the driver pulled from the front.

The driver was also our protector. There were bandits on the road.

We could not cover the distance in one day. A man walking steadily, without stopping, would have to walk for twelve hours to get to Modi'in. With and without the donkey's permission, we stopped now and again to eat, drink and rest for a while. As darkness came on, we looked for an inn to spend the night. I had always wondered what it would be like to sleep in an inn.

Now I know and do not care for it one bit. My mother and I were put in a room with two other women. One snored greatly, and I could not sleep. The inn was noisy, smelly and not too clean. I was glad when morning came and we could continue on our way.

We arrived in Modi'in late in the day, tired, dusty and hungry. The donkey driver and his animal went on their way.

When we entered the house I was happy to see bread and empty clay bowls waiting for us on Mattityahu's table. He received us warmly. His housekeeper led us to our room and brought us a basin of water. My mother and I spread our mats on the floor, washed and freshened ourselves. When I saw my mat spread out, I wanted to lie down and sleep. But I was hungry, and all I could think of was food.

Mattityahu joined my mother and me at the table. "I have already eaten," he said as the housekeeper filled our bowls with a wonderful-smelling bean soup. I brought the bowl to my lips and sipped.

A look from my mother told me I should not rush at my food. Mattityahu did not seem to mind.

"This has a wonderful flavor," my mother said to the house-keeper.

"I did not make it," she said, with a glance at Mattityahu. "The priest himself prepared it."

My mother looked at Mattityahu, astonished. I was also surprised.

"It is the one soup I know how to make," he said. "My wife, may she rest in peace, taught me. She was a wonderful cook."

It was hard for me to keep my eyes open, but I managed to eat everything that was put before me. I was grateful when Mattityahu saw how tired I was and sent me to bed.

The next day my mother and I walked about Modi'in to acquaint ourselves with the town. Houses of stone with flat wooden roofs were scattered around the town square. Mattityahu's house and those of his family face the town square. I met all the Hasmon children. There are no girls my age. One boy close to me in age is too shy to talk to me. Another is busy with his studies.

My father is my greatest disappointment. Each day he is supposed to come, and each day he does not come. There is much whispering in Mattityahu's study when his sons and the men of the town meet. I wonder if the whispering has something to do with the reason my father has not yet arrived. I asked my mother. She said, giving one of her famous answers, "When Father comes, we shall know all there is to know."

When my father did come, bringing me papyrus, he stayed for only one night. He seemed changed. He kissed my mother and me and went straight to our room to sleep for a while. When he got up, we all sat down to a fine meal of eggplant and onion, pomegranate juice and yogurt, prepared by Mattityahu's housekeeper. Then my father's news began to unfold.

"Antiochus' laws have served a good purpose," he said. "Many of his Jewish supporters resent the laws he passed and have come back to our side. Some have become fighters with Judah."

He smiled at me as he scooped up eggplant with his bread.

Mattityahu said, "I have received word that the battles have grown more intensive."

"And so they have," my father said. "Judah is in need of men, for fighting, patrolling, searching out the king's plans. We have spoken together, and I will be joining Judah's band."

I could not believe what my ears had heard. I looked at my mother, certain she would stop him. She said not a word.

"In the morning I leave for the hills," my father said, turning to me and taking my hand.

I began to cry.

"The fighting will not last forever," Mattityahu said.

Why does everyone think it is comforting to hear that a thing will not last forever? It is of no help at all.

I thought my mother would feel sorry for me. To my surprise she looked at me and said, "I never saw Rachel cry."

I withdrew my hand from my father's.

Mattityahu rose and went to his study. A feeling of shame came over me. Judah is his son—the same Judah I am so proud of. The same Judah who is fighting for my freedom, and my Jerusalem. My mother is right about Rachel. Her father has been away from home from the beginning of Judah's campaigns. I have never heard her complain.

"The more men Judah has, the more often his weary fighters can be sent home to rest for a few days," my father said. "The more fighters, the more often Rachel will be able to see her father." He said Rachel, but I knew he meant me.

"Look here," my father said, reaching into his sack and drawing out a sling for us to see.

"My first order from Judah—'practice stone slinging!' Come outside with me, and watch me practice."

I tried to look courageous as I went out with my mother and father.

"Where shall we go?" I asked.

"To the wood," my mother said.

The wood was beyond an olive grove, near the stream where I went for reeds. As we walked there, my father looked for, and found, stones of the right shape for a sling. In the wood at a

clearing, my mother and I seated ourselves on a rock. My father, performing for us, dropped the first stone before he could bring it to the sling.

"Your fingers are used to gold," my mother said. "They don't know what to make of stones."

"They'll soon learn," my father said, picking up the stone and placing it in the sling.

He swung his arm and sent out the stone, which fell at his feet. My mother and I tried not to laugh. I am glad to say, for the sake of our nation, that after a few more tries he managed to get one stone after another into the air.

9
A Lonely Time

My father left the next morning.

Mattityahu spends most of the day in his study by himself. Some days he teaches psalms and the words of the prophets to the people of the town. My mother and I always go to listen.

Now that we are in Mattityahu's house, his housekeeper has gone home to her family for a while. My mother and I keep busy, sweeping, cleaning, washing clothes, grinding flour to make bread, preparing meals. I go with the girls of the town to draw water from the well each morning, and again in the afternoon.

My mother pays no attention to my hair. Day after day it went uncombed—until the tangles so hurt my scalp, I asked her to braid it. From the look on her face, you would have thought I had given her a ruby.

The girls of the town are nice enough, but no one is as nice as Rachel. My mother has become friendly with some of the mothers. Some days she goes with me to the house of one girl or another, some days a girl and her mother come to us.

I go to the wood with the girls, or with Mattityahu's older grandchildren, to collect dry branches and twigs for the cookstove, or to pick wildflowers for my mother, or herbs for her to flavor soup with.

One day I found a perfect *marvah* plant and brought it home. My mother smiled sadly when she saw it. The plant was shaped like our Menorah, the seven-branch candelabrum that Antiochus stole from the Temple.

Mattityahu lets me use his study when he is not there. This afternoon as I sit in his room writing I hear my mother's sweet voice singing softly:

> *Jerusalem is empty.*
> *Her children do not go in or out.*
> *Her temple has been trampled by foreigners.*
> *Joy is gone.*

The words hurt. I long for Jerusalem. I even long for Rachel's pinches.

10

The Revolt

Then came *tohu v'vohu*, as our holy book calls it, a day dark and without form, like what existed before God began to make the world, except that this day was not silent. Cries, shouts and flashing swords split the air.

A messenger came to tell Mattityahu that the king's men were on the way to Modi'in. They were going from town to town, setting up altars, forcing Jews to sacrifice to Greek gods.

Modi'in is a small town. I remember Simon saying the king had no interest in small towns.

"I thought Modi'in was safe for Jews," I said.

"I thought so, too," my mother said.

"I know every soul in Modi'in," Mattityahu said. "They will respond with one voice."

He sent word of the news to his sons John, Eleazar, Yonatan and Simon. Midmorning, soldiers arrived. From our window we watched them move a statue of Zeus from a supply wagon and set it up in the square. They piled up stones to make an altar and added wood and twigs.

The officer, speaking through a tube, called out, "All residents of Modi'in, come to the square at once."

I was frightened enough and became even more frightened when my mother took me by the shoulder. I could feel her hand tremble, she who is not afraid of anything. With Mattityahu, we went to join the others of the town, standing in a half circle in the square.

"Bring the pig and fire," the officer called to his soldiers.

One soldier quickly slaughtered a pig behind the supply wagon. Another brought out fire in a copper lantern. He drew out a flame on a stick and touched it to the altar wood, kindling a fire.

I leaned forward to comfort myself with the sight of the Hasmon brothers, all big men and strong. My mother's hand on my shoulder pulled me back into line.

The officer went up to Mattityahu and said, "You are the priest Mattityahu?"

"I am," Mattityahu said.

"The king has a proposal for you," he said. "Sacrifice the pig to the god Zeus, and the king will honor you and your sons with a gold buckle for each, and much more besides."

Mattityahu grew stiff with anger. "God who made heaven and earth is our God," he said. "We sacrifice only to God."

To everyone's surprise, a man burst from the line, ran up to the officer and said, "I will sacrifice to Zeus."

I heard Mattityahu's voice cry, "Traitor!" Old as he was, he

rushed at the officer with the speed of an arrow, seized his sword and killed the man, then the officer. Then came the *tohu v'vohu*— wild shrieks, spears flying, swords flashing and the people of Modi'in running, shouting, throwing ashes, stones and blocks of wood at the soldiers.

As my mother pushed me into the house, I heard Mattityahu's voice cry, "Let everyone who is for God's teachings follow me."

I was still shaking, but my mother had grown calm.

"Gather your things," she said, making bundles. I did not have to ask why we were leaving. I knew Antiochus would seek revenge.

"Where will we go?" I asked, rolling up my sleeping mat.

"To my parents, in Yavne," she said.

"We need a donkey," I said.

"There is no shortage of donkeys in this country," my mother said, filling skins with water.

"How will Father know where we are?" I asked.

"Messengers will go between us. They will tell him and also let us know where he is."

I began to understand that my parents had made many decisions without my knowledge.

Into my rolled-up mat went the comb I never use, the mirror I never look into, the dice board and dice. I did not want to leave behind the scroll I had been writing on lest the king see it. Even my mother had no other suggestion. I rolled it up, slipped it into the mat and put the dry cake of ink in my pouch.

11

Yavne

We found a camel for hire before we found a donkey for our first day of walking. The driver took us only partway, leaving us at an inn when it began to grow dark. The next morning we found a donkey and continued on our way.

Yavne is a sandy village. Some people live in houses, some in tents. Before each house or tent is at least one sheep or goat. I asked my mother about a large stone court that we passed.

"It is a wine press," she said. "The people of the town bring their grapes here, to press into wine."

My grandmother and grandfather fell upon us with kisses when we arrived. Since then I have seen little of my grandfather. He is usually in his room, making copies of our sacred writing, though Antiochus has forbidden it. My grandmother tends the vineyard and fruit trees. My mother has taken over many of her duties in the house, and I help.

Nehemia, my mother's brother, is away in the hills. He is one of Judah's fighters. I am lonely in Yavne. I have two friends,

two sisters, one younger than me, one older. They live on the other side of the wine press. Their parents are strict. Sometimes I go to them, sometimes they come to me. Often their mother accompanies them and sits for a while, talking with my mother. I can see from my mother's face that the conversation does not interest her greatly.

The girls have told me they always have to give their mother an account of their time here when they come without her. They are asked, "Who else was there? What did you do? Did you eat something? What?"

The girls themselves are nice, but they have no wings.

"What do you mean?" my mother asked me when I said this to her.

I wasn't sure myself. "Rachel and I have wings," I said. "Jerusalem is a world, Yavne is a courtyard."

"Then you speak of Yavne, not of the girls," my mother said.

Since I was not certain myself what I meant, I said no more.

I have a lot of time to myself in Yavne, and have brought my scroll up to date.

Our house is busy. Judah's people come and go, bringing news of my father, of battles, of Jerusalem, and reports of dreadful happenings.

Our hearts stop to hear the tales of cruelty that are told. I cover my ears, so as not to hear, but the words seep through. It was not my plan to write them down, but my mother said, "Queen Esther did not leave anything out. If you are telling, tell."

It pains me to write this, but this is what the messengers report:

The king went to a town and ordered his men to round up all Jews. The Jews were led into a dark chamber. Lined up against a wall were whips, thumbscrews, iron claws, racks for breaking a person's back and a huge cauldron of boiling water. The king sat on a high chair. Beside him a soldier held a tray of meat.

"Who is your leader?" the king asked.

Eliezer, a priest, stepped forward.

"The meat in the tray is from a pig that has been sacrificed to the god Jupiter," the king said. "It is more delicious than usual. Taste it and see."

Eliezer answered, "Our law was established by God, who made heaven and earth. The law he gave us does not allow us to eat pig meat. We show our love for God by obeying his law."

"Foolish priest," the king said. "If you eat the meat, they will follow your example. You will save yourself and your people."

"I will not eat the flesh of a pig," Eliezer said.

The guards—I cannot bear to write this—seized Eliezer, whipped him till he bled, tied his arms to his sides and threw him into the cauldron.

I turn my head to shake the image from my mind. There is one more account.

In the chamber also were Hannah and her seven sons, all handsome young men. The king said to them, "The world is full of wonderful things. You will not get to see them if you do not eat this meat."

Hannah said to her sons, "Your dead father taught you the laws of Moses and the words of the prophets. Through this teaching you came to know God. Knowing God has given you joy in this world. The old priest endured great agony for God. Can you do less?"

One son after the other refused to eat. They broke the back of each one on the rack and threw him into the cauldron. Hannah leaped into the cauldron to die with her sons.

I was happy to leave my scroll to go with my mother and grandmother to buy oil. A merchant comes to the village once a month with a wagon.

Messengers who come from Jerusalem bring us news of the city and of Rachel's family. Rachel's house is a center for Judah's men. I hang on their every word and later always ask: How is Rachel? How did she spend the day? Who are her friends? I wonder if she misses me, but don't ask that. Their answer is always the same—"Rachel is well."

One messenger told us that Rachel's father had finished his work in Alexandria and was back home with his family. That's what he said, *finished his work in Alexandria,* when we all knew Rachel's father has been away in the hills with Judah. He also brought letters, one for my mother, one for me.

"From Rachel," he said, handing me a piece of broken pottery. She wrote: *I miss you. Soon we will all be together again.*

Rachel writes me short messages on pottery. I always have a

lot to say and write to her on papyrus if the messenger is return-
ing to Jerusalem.

One day a messenger came from the hills with mixed news. We
had lost a battle because our men would not fight back on the
Sabbath and break the law of Sabbath rest. Afterward,
Mattityahu made a new rule for Jews to follow. He said, "Life
comes first. Fight back with all your might." We also learned
from this messenger that our dear Mattityahu has died.

"Now write some good news," my mother said, reading over
my shoulder. She didn't have to tell me that. This is the good
news: The next battle was bigger than all the rest, and we won.

There was great excitement in Yavne. My grandmother
brought wine to the table. My grandfather left his room to dance
once around the table with us.

The best news of all is my father's arriving unexpectedly, with
my uncle Nehemia and with hugs and kisses.

12

Winter

When my mother finished hugging her brother, she looked at him and said, "Nehemia, what is that mark on your neck?"

Her mother and father came to look.

"It is nothing," Nehemia said, waving them away. "A wound that is healing."

"He was hurt in battle, but it is not serious," my father said. "I'm afraid we have much worse news."

We looked at him, waiting for him to say more.

"We are dusty from the road," my father said. "Let us wash first, and we will tell all."

He and Nehemia went to freshen themselves. Meanwhile, my mother and grandmother hurried to prepare a meal for them. I did my part. My mother mixed flour and water and kneaded dough. I rubbed stones to make fire and lit the kindling. When the stove was hot, I flattened the dough into patties and set them about the stove to bake.

I was in very good spirits. We had won the battle. Nehemia

had returned and my father was with us again. I already saw myself making bundles and going back to Jerusalem. I soon learned this was not to be.

We—my grandparents, my mother and I—had already eaten. But we sat down with my father and Nehemia, to keep them company as they ate.

"And the bad news?" my mother said.

My father looked at Nehemia.

"You tell them," Nehemia said, busy eating.

"There was another battle," my father said. "The king sent a large army against us that included war elephants."

I had never heard about war elephants and asked what these were.

My father explained. "On the back of each elephant is a cabin. In the cabin are men, soldiers."

"With swords and spears," Nehemia added. "And the elephants wear colorful sashes."

"The lead elephant wore royal colors, purple and gold," my father said. "Eleazar, Judah's brother, thinking the king was in the cabin, ran out to the fighting field and drove his sword into the animal's belly. It collapsed on top of him, killing him."

"He died for no reason," Nehemia said. "The king was not in the cabin."

We were silent around the table, with heavy hearts.

"Tell us about Judah," my grandfather said.

"He is a great man," my father said.

"A great leader," Nehemia said.

"What did he do to win your love?" my grandfather asked.

We all became interested.

"The sight of the king's army frightened us," my father said. "It was mighty, and well equipped. We were a handful of untrained fighters."

"I am not ashamed to say it," Nehemia said. "The sight was so terrible to us, we did not want to fight. But he always knew what to do. With gentle words he reminded us why we were fighting. With stronger words he asked us to remember the times our people met enemies mightier than ourselves and God came to our aid."

"And when he saw that his words had made us bold, he prayed and led us into battle," my father said.

I had never sat so long in my grandfather's company. He was usually in his room writing. Only on the Sabbath did he sit with us through the meal.

"Everyone now knows that the people began to call Judah 'the Maccabee,' and that the name has passed to all his fighters," my father said. "Judah was surprised when he learned of it."

"The word means Hammerer," my mother said, half to herself.

She told me that is what other nations call their heroes, and that is how we got the idea.

"In our case it means 'Hammer for God,'" my grandmother said.

"Even the king's men now call us 'Maccabees,'" Nehemia said.

"The word has a second meaning," my grandfather said. "It grows out of our ancient history, when Moses brought the Israelite slaves out of Egypt."

I know that story. It is one of those my mother tells. When Moses freed the slaves and took them out of Egypt, the Egyptians came running after them to take the slaves back to Egypt. But God parted the sea for the Israelites, and they crossed on dry land to safety.

"It comes from the song of thanksgiving that Moses sang," my grandfather said. "*Mi ka-mokha b'aylim Y*—'Who is like you among the gods?' Maccabee is made up of the first sound of each of those words."

I looked at my grandfather. I had never heard him say so much.

Now that my father had eaten and the conversation was over, I brought up my question. "When are we going back to Jerusalem?"

My mother and father glanced at each other, then turned to me.

"You and I are going somewhere," my mother said, "but not to Jerusalem."

My heart fell.

"Our victories have angered the king," my father said. "There is a rumor that he is preparing for a major battle. I must return, to be with Judah."

"Nehemia will remain here, to rest and recover," my mother said, reaching over to touch her brother's hand.

I did not like it. "Why can't Mother and I go back?"

"Have you forgotten?" my mother said. "We have put our house at the service of Judah. He needs it, for reasons of the war. Rachel's mother also serves the war."

Hearing Rachel's name was a stab in the heart.

My mother came over and kissed me on the head, trying to soothe me.

"It will not be long now before we can go back to Jerusalem," she said. "Now, with Nehemia back, there is no room for us here, but Father's cousins are in Alexandria, and we will go and stay in their house."

"Which cousins?" I asked, not caring.

"The ones in Jaffa," my mother said. "You will like Jaffa. It's on the sea. You have never seen the sea."

I didn't care if I ever saw the sea. Moon after moon, season after season, and still we do not return to Jerusalem.

13
Judah

We were preparing to leave for Jaffa when a messenger came with news. First he gave me a letter from Rachel, a piece of broken pottery on which she had scratched the words *Your jasmine tree misses you*. I carry her letters in my pouch and keep them close. Then the messenger sat down and gave us news of two battles.

My father's report was true. It was no rumor. Antiochus came out with a large army against the Maccabees. It was not my intention to write of these battles. When I told this to my mother, she fixed me with a Queen Esther look.

I took a new sheet of papyrus, wet my ink, sharpened a reed with a stone and began writing. I mean to cover only the main points.

The king's soldiers appeared on the fighting field wearing protective clothing and carrying spears, swords, shields. They had machines that shot arrows. Antiochus was so sure

of victory, he brought along slave auctioneers, to sell off his Jewish prisoners after the battle.

Our men had only slings, bows and arrows and bare arms to fight with.

Judah gave them heart.

"The king seeks to destroy our religion and separate us from God," he said. "Remember God's words to the Israelites: Five of you shall chase one hundred enemies, and a hundred of you shall chase ten thousand, and your enemies shall fall before you."

And he said, "Victory does not depend on the size of an army, for it comes from heaven."

"Lead us, Judah!" the men cried.

Judah bent his head in prayer:

God in heaven, scatter your enemies. Cause them to flee before you. As smoke is driven away, so drive them away. As wax melts before fire, so let the wicked perish. Make them like the whirling dust, as stubble before the wind, put shame on their faces, fill them with fear.

The battle began. Antiochus left in the middle to fight another war with Egypt. His men fought on. But not for long. Our men took aim and let go. No stone, no arrow, was wasted. Each found its mark. The king's men fled, leaving behind their swords, spears, helmets and other weapons, which the Maccabees were glad to get.

I don't mind writing of this second battle.

The victory of the Maccabees enraged Antiochus. He sent out another army. When his soldiers appeared on the battlefield, Judah said to his men, "I have a plan that will send them back this very night."

And that night his men set up tents and built fires, as if they were readying themselves for sleep. In fact they lay concealed nearby, watching and waiting. When they saw the soldiers steal into the camp with spears and swords to kill them, they hurried away to do their work. When the king's men arrived in the Israelite camp, they found it empty.

A greater surprise awaited them in their own camp. When they returned, they found smoke and ashes, and all the guards gone. The Maccabees had come while they were away and set fire to the camp.

· · ·

This is the start of a new scroll. I have done my Queen Esther-ly duty. My father has taken back to Jerusalem the writing I have done till now, to store in my chest. The word "chest" sends a picture to my mind that makes me happy. To stay longer and see more of my house in my thoughts, I add: "in my room, near my window, where my white wool dress waits for me."

My mother tells me, "It is good to speak of weather when writing a report."

She thinks I should mention the dry winter. Early in the season no rains fell. Trees and plants were parched. Then heavy rains came, watering the land. We will have wheat and barley to eat, and trees will be able to give generously of their fruit.

Nehemia has gone to the town square, to bring back a donkey and driver for us. My mother is calling to me. When the ink dries, I will roll up my sheet of papyrus and take it with me.

14
Jaffa

I have already written that Jaffa is on the sea. Those are words. They do not say that Jaffa is a fresh mist on the face, salty air, soft sounds of the sea lapping against the shore. I liked Jaffa so much, I began to feel like a traitor to Jerusalem. To Rachel also.

After my mother showed me the port where ships come in, she forbade me to go there. She says sailors are rough types. I don't care a fig for sailors, but I would have liked to watch ships come and go. Luck came along in the form of Rivka, a girl a year older than me who was born in Jaffa and knows every corner. She showed my mother and me a place not far from our house that is even more wonderful than the port. There are rocks to sit on that lead out into the sea. And fisher families.

The place met with my mother's approval. "But be careful on the rocks," she said.

Mornings, when I finish my household duties, I go with Rivka to the rocks. We sit with our feet dangling, enjoying the salty spray on our faces, and talk about our future husbands. She wants to marry the son of a fisher family. I can't think of anyone I want to marry. "Not even maybe?" she asked. I thought of Eliahu, who danced with the moon that dark and awful day. "Maybe Eliahu," I said, just to have a name.

We walk along the coast looking for stones for the dice board, which are easily lost, and watch small birds on little stick feet run up to the water and away from it. Rivka likes watching tiny crawling creatures pop out of the sand and back into it. I do not like these. Instead, I let my face feel the sea in the air.

Sometimes we spend time with the fisher families.

My mother told Rivka and me the story of the prophet Jonah, who spent three days in the belly of a great fish. The fish spat him up on the coast of Jaffa. We asked the fisher families if they knew where the whale spat Jonah up. They did not. So we walk along imagining that this place, or this one, was where Jonah landed.

I like Rivka, but she does not fill my heart the way Rachel did. Sometimes I call her Rachel by mistake. She does not like it, and tells me so. When I told my mother, she said, "People who live near the sea are outspoken." As I have already written, my mother sometimes says strange things. When she looked over my shoulder and read these words, she pulled my braid and said, "She lives near the sea, does she not? And did you yourself not tell me she speaks her mind?"

It is hard to win an argument with my mother.

The best thing about Jaffa is that my father is often with us. Our side is driving back Antiochus' armies. We are winning the war. The more victories the Maccabees have, the more men come to join Judah. He has plenty of fighters.

One day a messenger came to tell us that my father would be home for the Sabbath.

"I will make a banquet," my mother said.

I looked at her. Our usual meal was vegetable soup, greens dipped in olive oil, bread and lentil patties. We drank goat's milk and pomegranate juice. I waited for an explanation.

"I will bake a quail for the Sabbath meal," she said.

"And where will you get quail?"

"From the same place Moses got quail," she said.

I did not know how she would manage it, but I knew what she meant. Moses freed the Israelite slaves in Egypt and brought them out to the desert wilderness. They complained about the poor food they had to eat. Moses asked God for help, and God caused quail to come flying into the Israelite camp.

"This is not the desert wilderness," I said.

"The desert wilderness is everywhere," she said.

I thought no more about what she had said and went with my dice and dice board to play with Rivka. When I came home, I found my mother dressing a bird. I was as surprised as the Israelites must have been.

Rubbing the bird with oil, she said, "It is good there will be a full moon tonight. This is almost the last of the oil. I have set the remainder aside, for Father to cleanse himself. But we have none to kindle the Sabbath lights."

My thoughts were on the mystery of the bird. "Is it a quail?" I asked.

"A cousin," she said. "Come, let us bake bread."

We became busy, cleaning, pounding, baking, setting the Sabbath table; and as the sun began to set, a dusty and wild-looking man—my father—walked in. He greeted us from the door, then went to wash. Soon he came to the table wearing a fresh garment, combed, smelling of cloves and looking handsome again.

He stood over the banquet table admiring the spread: bread, a bowl of greens, the quail's roasted cousin, a pitcher of pomegranate juice. He looked at the oil lamps on the table, their wicks showing but unlit.

"We do not have enough oil to kindle the Sabbath lights," my mother said. "But come with me—we will bless the Sabbath lights in another way."

We followed her out.

A full moon shone in the sky, and around her, her many children, the stars, twinkled and winked.

My mother gazed up at them. "There are our kindled lights," she said. She closed her eyes and recited the Sabbath blessing as if she were reciting it over flames that she had kindled herself. My

father and I fell in with her intention, saying, "Good Sabbath," when she was through.

Inside, sitting around the table, with a full moon at the window lighting up the room, we sat talking and eating, happy to be together. The smell of the sea, the sound of water rolling softly up to the shore, filled me with happiness. Nothing was usual about that night, starting with the quail's cousin. That night, for the first time in a long time, I felt the full meaning of the word we used to greet each other: *shalom*—at peace.

15

Summer

The next morning someone came from the port with a letter from my father's cousins in Alexandria, in whose house we were, with wonderful news.

First the letter. They said they were staying on in Egypt, and we should give the key to the house, when we leave, to Rivka's mother. They wrote that Alexandria had beautiful buildings, schools, a great library—which contained also our holy books—gardens, zoos and a museum. I was stunned. We were amazed when we learned that the streets of Rome were paved, so wheels or horses' hooves could not sink in mud in the rainy season. But Alexandria! I had never heard of such marvels.

The news was this. I will write exactly the words that came to our ears: "Antiochus has called a truce. The fighting is over."

"Can it be true?" my mother asked.

"That is what they say," the man said.

As my parents spoke between themselves, I thought of my return to Jerusalem. Waves of happiness washed over me as I saw myself walking through the courtyard gate, into the courtyard, past the jasmine tree, toward Rachel's door.

I was too excited to sit still, and jumped up.

"Where are you going?" my mother asked.

"To gather my belongings," I answered.

"Not yet," my father said. "I will leave first, and you and Mother will follow."

"When?" I asked.

"Very soon," my mother said. "A day or two."

I had been away from Jerusalem and Rachel for so long, I could wait another day or two. I was in high spirits at the idea of leaving and went happily about, sweeping and dusting in the house, washing and drying clothes, setting things in order, saying good-bye to Rivka and the fisher families two and three times.

My mother and I set out early on a clear day, with donkey and driver, walking until darkness fell, stopping at an inn, continuing in the morning. In this land news travels swiftly, as if on eagle wings, and good and bad news followed us.

As we entered the first inn, we learned that the king had lied about a truce. He had sent a surprise army to wipe out the Maccabees. We worried half the night and could think of little else. The next day, at the second and last inn, we were awakened in the middle of the night by shouts and laughter. When we opened the door, we heard people congratulating themselves and one another. A man had delivered news that the king had wearied of making war and had called for a real truce. We heard the man read a copy of the letter of regret the king had written to his troops.

This was what his letter said:

I did evils in Jerusalem. I set out to destroy a people without good reason. The Jews do not consent to become Greek. They prefer their own way of living. Let their Temple be restored to them, and let them follow the customs of their ancestors.

It seems the general who read the king's letter aloud to the troops added his own words.

Why did this people rise up against us? Because we did not let them practice their religion. Let us make peace with them and allow them to live as they see fit.

In my excitement to write this, my point has broken. I must take a new reed pen.

At last, the war with Antiochus is truly over. Thank God for that.

As I finish writing, I hear the bray of a donkey outside. A donkey's bray is not a pleasant sound, but I have come to love it. Each hoarse call means we are moving on and coming closer to Jerusalem.

My heart hammers against my chest. I will write more from Jerusalem.

16

My Jasmine Tree

The journey to Jerusalem was hot and tiring. We did not mind. We were happy. My mother sang love songs to God. Even the donkey was in a good mood, walking with a lively step. The driver left us at the gates of Jerusalem, and my mother and I went on alone, walking beside the donkey. I could not hear anything for the banging in my chest. I wondered if I was going to die. Entering the courtyard gate, I thought I would faint.

There stood Rachel and her family, with smiling faces. My father came hurrying down the steps.

I could not move or speak. Rachel put her arms around me and held me. Then came the kissing, hugging and glad faces wet with tears. I could not bring myself to let go of Rachel long enough to even look at her.

"Alexandra, there are others here to greet," my mother said.

Crying with happiness, I let go of Rachel and went to hug her mother, her father and Boaz. Then I went back to Rachel.

"Come," my father said, removing bundles from the donkey's back. "I have made a fire in the grate—the house is warm."

My mother followed him up the steps, and Boaz went with her, taking up the remaining bundles.

"Bathsheba," Tamar called to my mother, "I have food for you. Boaz will bring up bread and soup."

"And I will bring this fellow back to its owner," Rachel's father said, leading the donkey out of the courtyard.

Boaz was soon down again, and going up once more with a pot of soup and bread.

Rachel and I stood holding hands while facing each other. She was the same—neat, each hair in place.

"You haven't changed, Rachel," I said. "And I am covered with dust."

"You've been traveling," she said. "Otherwise you're the same, too."

There was something new in her face, but I didn't know what.

"Maybe you did change, a little—" I said.

"You did, too, a little," she said.

I felt a bit uncomfortable, I did not know why. I reached around for my braid and waved it at her. "Same braid," I said.

Boaz came down and joined us.

"You have changed very much, Boaz," I said.

"I'm eight years old," he said. "I went alone to watch the workers at the Temple today," he added.

The Temple! I had almost forgotten.

"Let us go see it," I said.

"It's getting dark," Rachel said. "Besides, there's nothing to

see. Donkeys and porters carrying loads, carpenters banging on boards, stonemasons hammering away."

I looked at her. I had forgotten. The Temple that had come to my mind was before Antiochus.

Rachel saw my confusion. "The Temple was in ruins when Judah took it back," she said. "Antiochus' soldiers lived there. They made fires and cooked and let pigs run wild. Tall grass covered the courtyard. The stones were black with smoke—"

I thought of the beautiful stones. "Beige stones that turn gold in the sunset," I said sadly.

"Alexandra!" my mother called from our doorway.

"I'm coming," I said.

"We'll go to the Temple tomorrow morning," Rachel said.

"Wait till the twenty-fifth of Kislev," Boaz said. "Our Temple will be beautiful again."

The date was familiar. "Wasn't that when Antiochus polluted our Temple?" I said.

"The very reason Judah chose it to rededicate the Temple to God," Rachel said. "It will be a great celebration."

"Priests, Temple musicians, all Temple officials left Jerusalem when the Temple was destroyed," Boaz said. "Judah's brothers are going around the country bringing them back."

For a moment I had forgotten why they had left, then remembered. Their duties centered on Temple ceremonies. With the Temple destroyed, they had no work.

"Judah," I said, half to myself, feeling love for the man who had saved our ways and customs and returned our Temple to us again.

"Prince Judah! That's what we now call him," Rachel said, looking proud. "Important men come from Rome to see him."

It was a great deal to take in all at once. I suddenly felt tired. The night air chilled me. My thoughts went to the bowl of soup waiting for me.

"I'm hungry," I said, heading for the stairs.

"Golden dreams," Rachel called after me.

I waved a little wave, too tired to speak.

A quiet joy washed over me as I entered my house. A fire burning in the grate warmed the room. Wicks burned in clay lamps around the walls. On the table was a large bowl filled with pomegranates, dried apricots, raisins, walnuts, pistachios, almonds and fig cakes.

"To welcome you home," my father said.

"Wash the dust from yourself and come and eat," my mother said, ladling soup into a bowl.

I went into my room to wash and saw that my father had unrolled my sleeping mat on the floor and thrown a blanket and pillow over it. I opened the shutter to look out. A full moon lit up the courtyard. Points of light danced on the leaves of the jasmine tree. I glanced again at the sleeping mat.

That is all I remember of that night.

17

A New Menorah

My mother, my father and I were happy at our morning meal. We did not say much. It was enough, the joy we felt at being together in our own home, in the peaceful streets of Jerusalem. That morning I swept and cleaned and fetched water, filling my basin and my parents'. My father went to his shop in the market. My mother took her loom to the open door, to have light, and began weaving. It was as if we had never been away. I glanced around, reacquainting myself with our oil lamps, pots, cushions, the portable stove—still and silent old friends.

"Alexandra!" called Rachel.

My heart leapt at the sound. Excited, I went to the door.

"Where are you going?" my mother asked.

"To visit the Temple," I said.

"Wait till your father comes home—he will take you."

Her words puzzled me. She often said strange things. But the sound of amusement was missing from her voice.

"I'm not a child to need a father to take me," I said.

"That is the point," my mother said. "A Jerusalem maiden of marriageable age does not walk alone in the streets."

She had never spoken to me of Jerusalem maidens of marriageable age before. Why now?

"I will not be alone—I will be with Rachel," I said.

"Even the two of you together should not go about, except in the company of an older brother, a parent or relative."

My mother had become a stranger overnight.

"I do not have an older brother," I said.

"Ask Rachel if Josef can accompany you both," she said.

Another surprise. "Who is Josef?" I asked.

"Rachel's friend," my mother said. "His family lives downstairs, where Simon used to live."

When had my mother learned this? Was it when she and Tamar had spoken together in the courtyard, yesterday? Had Tamar come up after I had fallen asleep and talked to her?

Rachel called my name again.

Glad to end the conversation, I went to the window.

"I'm on my way," I called down.

"Ask her," my mother said, coming up behind me.

I looked at my mother, the stranger.

"Ask her," she repeated.

"My mother wants to know if Josef can accompany us," I said.

"He's in the study house," Rachel answered.

"Well—go along this time," my mother said.

I hurried down the steps to the courtyard, glad to leave.

Rachel and I hugged each other. "Just like before," she said.

We heard a door open and turned to see a woman come from the house where Simon had lived.

"Good morning, girls," she said, passing us.

"Good morning, my lady," we answered, like proper Jerusalem maidens.

"Josef's mother," Rachel whispered as the woman left.

I looked at Rachel. I was beginning to see what was different about her. And to understand my mother's sudden stiffness.

"Is Josef a new friend?" I asked.

"He's not so new anymore," Rachel said.

"Is he somebody special?" I asked.

"Maybe," she said with a grin.

We both laughed at her answer, then linked arms the way we used to and walked out onto the street.

Not only did Rachel have a new friend, Jerusalem also seemed changed.

"I see new faces," I said, looking about as we walked along. "That house is new. Stones have been added to raise that courtyard wall."

"They are already old to me," Rachel said.

"I like most what I don't see," I said.

"What do you mean?"

"I don't see Antiochus' soldiers. Statues of Greek gods. Jewish boys in Hermes hats. Gold buckles . . ."

"No," Rachel said softly. "Jerusalem is ours again."

"Alexandra!" a voice called.

I turned.

Eliahu, who had danced with the moon so long ago, came hurrying up to us. He looked different. Did he always have curly brown hair?

"I thought it was you," he said.

"Eliahu!" I said, glad to see him. "How did you know me from the back?"

"The braid," he said. "And Rachel, walking beside you."

I was glad to see him and borrowed my mother's words to try to keep him with us.

"My mother says Jerusalem maidens mustn't walk alone. Will you accompany us to the Temple?" I said, but I left out the "of marriageable age" part.

"I regret that I cannot," he said. "Our relatives are coming from Egypt and we are building an extra room for them. I must help with the work."

"Do they mean to live here?" Rachel asked.

"We don't know," Eliahu said. "For now, they are coming to experience free Jerusalem, and for the rededication ceremony."

I did not want him to go, but there was no way to keep him with us.

"We will meet again soon," he called, hurrying off.

Rachel and I walked on to the Temple.

What she and Boaz had said was true. There was nothing to see, only laborers, porters and donkeys. Loose boards and stones lay about everywhere. Rachel saw my disappointment.

"One place is more finished," she said. "Follow me."

I followed her, climbing over stones and boards to a hill.

"Lean this way, and you can see the Holy Place," she said.

The sight took my breath away. Our treasures that Antiochus had stolen had been replaced. There was a new show table, a new incense altar and a new Menorah, its seven branches like seven arms reaching up to heaven.

"Oh, Rachel!" I said.

"The Menorah is smaller than the one Antiochus stole, and it's not golden—" Rachel said.

"I don't care. It's beautiful," I said, on the point of tears.

"I know," she said, tears rising in her own eyes.

We headed home, feeling happy, and passed two women talking excitedly about a miracle.

"What miracle?" I asked.

"They found a vial of holy oil in the Temple," a woman said.

"It cannot be," Rachel said. "There have been no priests to make holy oil for three years."

"That is the wonder," the woman said. "The oil is from three years ago. It still bears the seal of the high priest."

Rachel and I stared at each other. Now that was a miracle. Something to blow the horn about.

Two Jerusalem maidens of marriageable age forgot about modesty and ran home like children to bring their mothers the news.

I have not shown my mother what I have written here, and she has not asked to see it. I don't think she would like being called a stranger.

18
The Twenty-fifth of Kislev 3595

Fig trees and date palms gave their fruit, pomegranates ripened on the trees, summer passed and winter came to the land, bringing the month of Kislev. There is a saying for this month: *Cold in the morning, cold at night and hot when the sun shines. The ox shivers at dawn but looks for shade at noon.* My mother, the stranger, has become strict about young Jerusalem maidens alone in the streets of Jerusalem. On dry days, when our work in the house is over, Rachel and I go to the market. Or to the Temple, to see how the work is progressing. Sometimes Josef accompanies us, sometimes Eliahu of the curly hair.

Then came the great day, the twenty-fifth of Kislev. The air crackled with excitement. The streets were crowded. People came from Egypt, Cyprus, Rhodes, even from Greece and Italy, across the Mediterranean, to be present for the dedication ceremony.

My mother looked beautiful in the new yellow robe and velvet headband she had made for herself. Every step she took gave off a scent of lavender, her favorite dusting powder. My father had trimmed and oiled his beard, and he looked handsome in a new tunic.

I smelled nice, too, as I dusted myself with my mother's powder. But I cannot say I looked my best. My mother had offered to make a new robe for me, but I insisted on wearing my old white holiday robe, which had lain in the chest for so many moons.

"It's too short," my mother said when I put it on.

"I like it this way," I said, not meaning it.

"It's too tight," my mother said.

"It's the way I'm standing," I said, twisting my body as I went from the room.

Though I looked strange from the neck down, I believe that from the neck up . . . But I must stop there. As a modest Jerusalem maiden, I may say no more. I will let it come out when I report later what Rachel had to say when she saw me.

"Three blasts, calling us to the Temple!" my father cried.

The sound always gave me a chill. Since ancient times a blast on the shofar, the ram's horn, has been the rallying cry of our people.

I ran to the window to see if Rachel was yet in the courtyard. When I saw the top of her head crossing the courtyard, I pulled away. I wanted to see the look of surprise on her face when she saw me.

"I'm going down," I said, taking my wrap, a shawl my mother had woven for me.

Rachel, hearing my door click open, looked up. Her eyes opened wide and her hand flew to her face as she watched me walk down the steps.

"What?" I said, trying not to laugh.

"Your braid—it's gone," she said.

My hair, which had been imprisoned in a braid, hung loose around my shoulders. A velvet band like my mother's circled my forehead.

"My mother wanted to cut it off, and I let her," I said, enjoying Rachel's surprise.

Rachel stood staring at me, her hand at her cheek, as if it would fall off if she let go. When Boaz and Josef came out and also stared, saying nothing, I began to wonder if I looked strange from the neck up as well.

Boaz broke the silence. "I never knew you had so much hair," he said.

"You look pretty," Josef said.

Rachel let go of her face. "Pretty?" she said. "She looks beautiful."

I felt myself grow red with embarrassment. "Rachel!" I said, and began tugging at my robe. I could not make it longer, but I succeeded in taking attention away from my hair.

"Another blast!" Josef said as the ram's horn sounded.

From upstairs and down, our families, all in holiday dress, filled the courtyard and were

soon out on the street marching to the Temple. I walked a little ahead of Rachel and Josef, enjoying the sight of happy, well-dressed people, looking to see if Eliahu might be among them.

As we entered the Temple plaza, we saw Judah standing off to one side. He no longer looked like a desert dweller but like a prince, as Rachel had said. People bowed to him as they passed. I was proud when he came over to talk to our parents.

"You made this night possible, Judah," my father said.

"We all did," Judah said, taking my father's hand and Micah's between his own two hands.

"You should be up on a high step, wearing purple and gold," my mother said.

"I am happy enough here in the shadows, seeing joy on people's faces," Judah said.

We parted with Judah and entered the crowded Temple court. I felt tears come to my eyes when I saw priests ascending and descending the altar ramp. The sight of sacrifices on the altar being offered up to God had been missing from our lives since Antiochus' laws drove us from Jerusalem. I looked at my parents. They were also teary.

I felt a jab in my side. It hurt, but I said nothing. I remembered how much I had missed Rachel's jabs, and pinches, while I was away. I wondered if she jabbed Josef to get his attention.

"The Menorah!" she whispered.

I looked and saw seven wicks, burning in seven cups. "What?" I asked, not understanding.

"Which cup has the holy oil?" she said.

I had forgotten about the vial of oil that had been found. I did not wonder about it for long. A long trumpet blast struck the air, bringing priests in white robes marching out on a high step. They turned to face us. The singers followed, in their white robes, then the musicians with their harps, lutes and cymbals.

I turned to Rachel, but she was talking to Josef. I looked about for Eliahu. He was surely there, but the crowd was too great to find anyone. Remembering the fit of my robe, I was glad not to find him.

Sweet harp notes filled the air, then a clash of cymbals. Priests with palm branches came marching out onto the court. Waving their branches, they made seven circles around the court, singing a song written by King David: *"All praise to you, our God, creator of heaven and earth, for the miracle of victory and for not letting our enemies rejoice over us."*

"Doesn't it make you glad?" I said to Rachel.

"I love it," she said, her eyes on the palm priests.

The choirmaster gave a signal, and musicians lifted their instruments and played as the choir sang, *"Hallelujah, hallelujah. Praise God with gladness for allowing us once more to stand in the house of God."*

My mother, behind me, sang along with them.

One love song to God followed another. When the singing was over, everyone fell silent. The priests were about to give the priestly blessing.

Reciting first the words that gave them permission to bless, they said, *"Praise God who commanded Aaron, the first priest, in whose place we stand, to bless the people of Israel with love."* Then they raised their arms, touching thumbs together.

I lowered my head to receive the blessing and saw Rachel's sandals move closer to mine.

Speaking with one voice, the priests chanted, *"May God bless you and protect you. May God be gracious to you. May God lift up his face to you and grant you peace."*

I could almost feel God's blessing travel down to me along the priests' outstretched arms.

We raised our heads and looked at each other with happiness.

Saying nothing, we turned and went from the Temple square.

My father and Micah saluted Judah as we left. As we walked away, both fathers cried suddenly, *"Judah, Judah, king of Israel."* Everyone took up the cry, filling the air with shouts of *"Judah, Judah, king of Israel."*

And whose voice stood out? Her voice—who had strong opinions about how a proper Jerusalem maiden should behave—was heard above the rest.

19
The Sabbath Wood

I unroll my papyrus to write on it for the last time. The days I chose to write about are over. A detail of the Maccabee story remains. Remember the vial of holy oil that was found? Oil that was supposed to burn for only one day? It burned for eight days! Rachel and I saw it with our own eyes. People said it was a miracle. And so it was. To my mind, the greater miracle was Judah's. With a handful of untrained Maccabees he defeated Antiochus' army and won back Jerusalem for us.

To engrave these happenings in the memory of our people, Judah and the elders sent letters to Jews around the world setting forth the events and saying: *Mark the twenty-fifth day of Kislev as the start of an eight-day holiday.*

With those words creating a new holiday, that story ends—and mine begins. I will not write of it, but only of one day in the Sabbath wood, this day.

Our meal was over. My parents, and all parents in Jerusalem, were asleep, enjoying the Sabbath rest. Jerusalem itself seems to go to sleep after the noonday meal on the Sabbath. It is so silent, you can hear the city breathe.

I believe Moses dropped a commandment when he brought the ten down from Mount Sinai. There must have been an eleventh that said, *You shall not disturb the rest of sleepers on the Sabbath.*

The wooden comb and hand mirror that my mother gave me many and many moons ago now receives much use. My hair combed, wearing my Sabbath robe, I stood at my window inhaling the sweet scent of jasmine and watching for Rachel. On the Sabbath she could not call up to me and wake the sleepers.

I saw her cross the courtyard, turn and motion for me to come down. I nodded, a little too wildly, to enjoy the sensation of my hair brushing against my cheek. I tiptoed past my sleeping parents and out the door.

As I went down to the courtyard, Josef came from his house. Without exchanging a word, we three passed quietly from the courtyard, out to the street, heading for the wood. To admire God's handiwork, as my mother would say. And also to laugh and talk freely, without fear of waking anyone.

As we climbed up to the two boulders near a fig tree, where we liked to sit, friends we passed called "Good Sabbath," and we answered back. The wood smelled of wild rosemary. It was spring, and the ground was covered with red poppies, anemones and other wildflowers in bloom.

I made myself comfortable on my boulder. Rachel and Josef seated themselves opposite me.

"Rachel," Josef said, nodding up the hill. "There's your little brother."

"So I see," Rachel said, looking up at Boaz talking with his friends.

"He used to want to be with Rachel and me all the time," I said. "Now he takes no notice of us."

"That is how it is when boys grow up," Josef said. "And here comes our fourth," he added, nodding downhill.

Eliahu came hurrying up, a folded cloth in his hand. It made me happy to see him.

"What is he carrying?" Rachel asked.

"We'll soon know," I said.

I moved over on the boulder to make room for Eliahu. He opened the cloth and held it up to us. "Poppy-seed cakes—one for each," he said.

I saw only three as I took one. "None for you?" I asked.

"I am sick of them," he said, shaking the cloth free of crumbs. "My Egyptian aunt is queen of poppy-seed cakes. Every Friday she bakes a year's supply."

I laughed at the exaggeration.

"My mother's are better," Rachel said, eating. "Aren't they, Alexandra?"

As it was Eliahu's aunt and not his mother who had done the baking, I answered truthfully, "They are."

We—my parents and I—have met Eliahu's relatives. Next week they are coming to us for the Sabbath meal. My father's relatives—the ones from Jaffa, in whose house my mother and I stayed—will also be there. My mother no longer speaks of how Jerusalem maidens should behave. She now speaks of the duties of a wife and the obligations of a husband. She is so serious, I almost laugh, listening to her. She used to be so lighthearted.

"You can expect them to bring some poppy-seed cakes to your house when they come, Alexandra," Eliahu said. "Be careful what you say."

"I will eat two at a time and make noises of enjoyment," I said.

Eliahu turned to tell Rachel and Josef about his relatives. I love the wood, and I looked away as they spoke, glancing about. Overhead, the sky was clear, as blue as a high priest's tassel. Around us were olive trees. A pomegranate tree was already in bloom. Listening to Eliahu's voice, and enjoying the red poppies and anemones that covered the ground, I felt a wave of great happiness wash over me. It made me cry. Bending down so no one would notice my tears, I pinched off an oregano leaf and brought it to my nose to smell it.

"Quiet, everyone," Eliahu said. "Alexandra is praying."

They laughed, and I laughed with them. I had told them what my mother used to say, when we went to gather herbs: *Smell the plant, show God you enjoy the world he made for us—it is a form of prayer.*

All this I have written sitting on a pillow in front of the chest in my room, with my papyrus roll resting on the chest. I lift more ink on the tip of my pen to write the last words. It is always a little sad to finish something. My mother says there is nothing to be sad about; one thing finishes and another begins. So be it. I will leave the ink to dry and go to my window to breathe in the sweet scent of jasmine.

When the ink is dry, I will roll up my papyrus and put it in the chest with the other sheets. Then I will go into the next room to sit with my mother and father and speak with them about poppy-seed cakes.

Afterword

The holiday of Hanukkah, which Judah and the elders created, commemorates two events: the success of the Maccabees in winning back Jerusalem, allowing Jews to live in freedom and sacrifice to God on a purified altar; and the miracle of the oil—one vial burning for eight days.

Hanukkah, a Hebrew word that means rededication (of the Temple), begins on the twenty-fifth of Kislev, which falls in November/December, and lasts eight days. It is celebrated in the home with gladness—lighting candles and giving thanks.

A special nine-branch candelabra has been brought into being for the celebration. It is called a *hanukkiah*. The ninth cup is a service station. It holds a "worker" candle. The worker is lit first. With its flame all the candles are lit—one on the first night, two on the second, and so on—until all eight candles have been lit, and nine burn brightly. The custom is to set the hanukkiah in the window, so its lights, conveying celebration, may be seen from the street. Another name for the holiday is Festival of Lights.

Friends and family come together each night to light candles, sing songs and eat holiday foods. Children receive as presents "gold coins"—chocolate disks wrapped in gold foil—and other small gifts.